WRITER: ALESSANDRO SISTI PENCILS: VALENTINO FORLINI INKS: SONIA MATRONE COLORS: GIORGIO VALLORANI LETTERS: MICHAEL STEWART

IT'S FINE! IT JUST NEEDS--
COME ON, DOC! DON'T BE SUCH A GRUMP!
DO YOU THINK STANLEY LIKES LOOKING AT THIS OLD THING ALL DAY?
IT WOULD BE UNPATRIOTIC NOT TO REPAINT IT!
IT WOULD BE GOOD FOR BUSINESS!
WE'VE GOTTA PAINT ANOTHER ONE!
RAMONE CAN DO IT!
MY HUSBAND IS THE BEST ARTIST AROUND.
YOU CAN COUNT ON ME!
WHAT DO YOU SAY, SALLY?
WELL, UH... I AGREE WITH THEM!

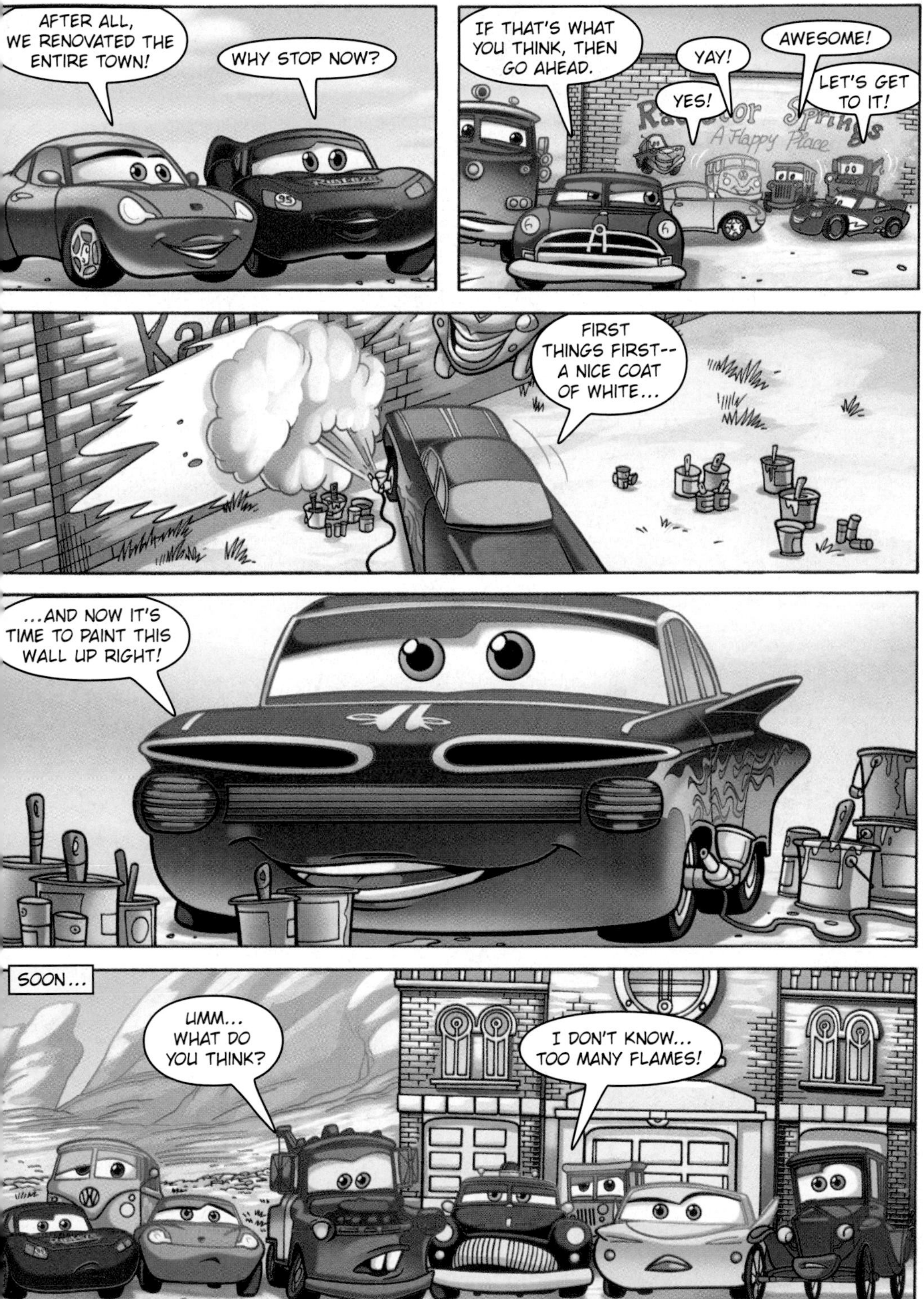
AFTER ALL, WE RENOVATED THE ENTIRE TOWN!
WHY STOP NOW?
IF THAT'S WHAT YOU THINK, THEN GO AHEAD.
YES!
YAY!
AWESOME!
LET'S GET TO IT!
Radiator Springs A Happy Place
FIRST THINGS FIRST-- A NICE COAT OF WHITE...
...AND NOW IT'S TIME TO PAINT THIS WALL UP RIGHT!
SOON...
UMM... WHAT DO YOU THINK?
I DON'T KNOW... TOO MANY FLAMES!

RAMONE, CAN YOU ADD SOME BUMBLEBEES?
I LIKE BUMBLEBEES.
PUT IN SOMETHING THAT WILL LET PEOPLE KNOW THIS IS A PLACE OF PEACE AND ORGANIC LIVING.
BUT ALSO A PLACE OF PATRIOTS AND GOOD MORALS!
GROAN
OK, IF YOU KNOW IT ALL, WHY DON'T YOU HELP ME?
GIVE ME SOME PAINT, HOTSHOT!
I'LL HELP YA, HONEY!
THERE CAN NEVER BE TOO MANY FLOWERS!
AND STARS!
AND A LOT OF RED, WHITE, AND BLUE!
ART WAS BETTER BACK IN THE '20S!

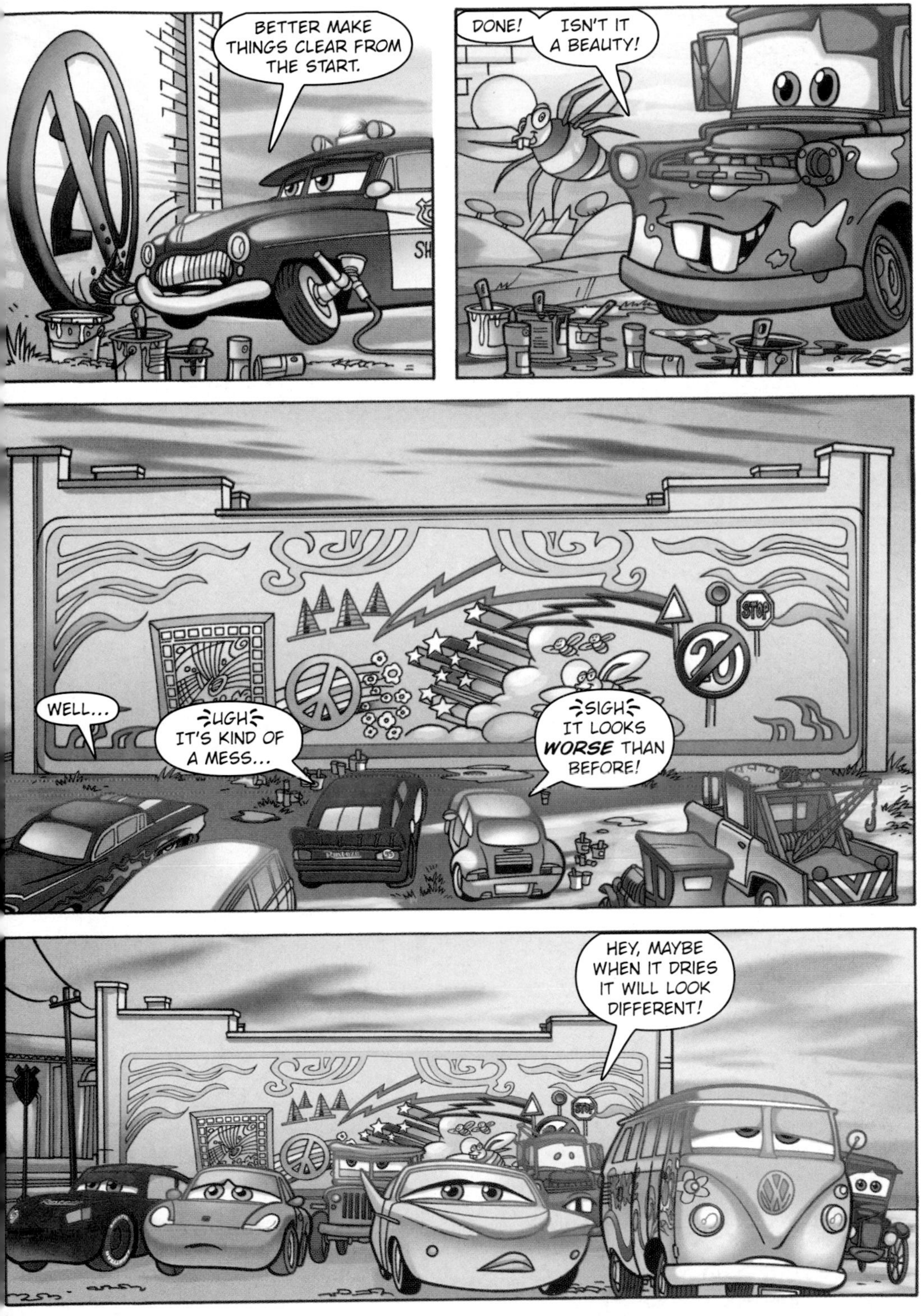

BETTER MAKE THINGS CLEAR FROM THE START.
DONE!
ISN'T IT A BEAUTY!
SH
STOP
WELL...
UGH IT'S KIND OF A MESS...
SIGH IT LOOKS WORSE THAN BEFORE!
HEY, MAYBE WHEN IT DRIES IT WILL LOOK DIFFERENT!

COME ON, *RED,* THEY'VE ALL GONE!

NOW IT'S *OUR* TURN TO DO SOME PAINTING.

THE NEXT MORNING...
OOOH, STANLEY-- LOOK!

Radiator Springs
A Happy Place
OUR DEAR OLD MURAL.
PERFECTLY RESTORED!
I TOLD YA IT WOULD LOOK BETTER AFTER IT DRIED.
AS I SAID, IT JUST NEEDED A LITTLE FRESHENING UP!
THANKS, DOC!
YOU'RE ALWAYS THE BEST JUDGE...
...AND ART CRITIC!
THE END!

Disney • PIXAR
THE WORLD OF Cars

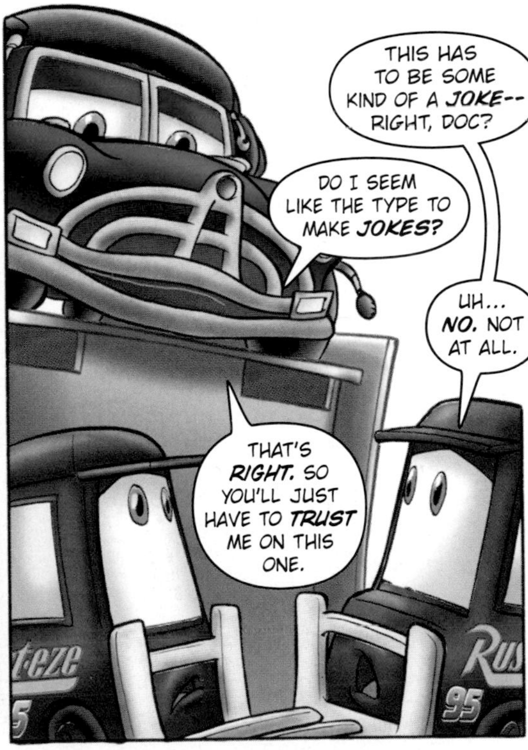

WRITER: MICHAEL STEWART ART: VALENTINO FORLINI LETTERS: MICHAEL STEWART

LATER, LIGHTNING MCQUEEN HAS A COMMANDING LEAD IN THE RACE...
SPEED! I AM SPEED!
YOU'RE DOING GREAT, KID. BUT IT'S TIME FOR A PIT STOP.
ALL RIGHT, DOC! BUT THERE ARE ONLY FIVE MORE LAPS LEFT--I THINK I CAN MAKE IT!
YEAH-- THAT'S WHAT YOU ALWAYS SAY.
OKAY, MATER, GO OUT THERE AND SHOW 'EM WHATCHA GOT.
YOU GOT IT, DOC!
NOW YOU FELLERS ARE GONNA SEE WHAT A "RUSTY OLD TOW TRUCK" CAN DO!
KA-CHOW!
HUH?
THIS IS JUST LIKE BEING AT THE FISHIN' HOLE BACK HOME!
MCQUEEN'S ACTUALLY COMING IN FOR A PIT STOP!
WELCOME BACK TO THE PIT CREW!
WAY TO GO, MATER!
YOU STILL GLAD TO HAVE HIM ABOARD, HOT ROD?
UH... WELL, I...
FABULOUS HUDSON HORNET 51
AW, SHOOT. YOU'RE GONNA MAKE ME BLUSH!
THE END!

WRITER: ALESSANDRO SISTI PENCILS: FABIO POCHET INKS: RAFFAELLA SECCIA COLORS: GIORGIO VALLORANI LETTERS: JOHN GREEN

HOW CAN HE BEAT ME? I'M A RACE CAR!
YEAH, HE IS A... UH... A "PRE-CISIONAL INSTRUMENT OF SPEED AND AERO-MATICS".
WELL, SO WHAT?
YOU WANT A CHALLENGE? YOU AND I, THE SAME ROAD AS LAST TIME!
FROM THE HIGHWAY BILLBOARD TO THE TELEPHONE POLES.
JUST TRY NOT TO DESTROY ANYTHING THIS TIME.
C'MON, SHERIFF... I DON'T WANT TO EMBARRASS YOU.
OH, WELL, IF YOU'RE NOT UP FOR IT...
OK, IF YOU PUT IT THAT WAY, I ACCEPT!
ATTABOY! THERE'S JUST ONE MORE DETAIL...

THE RACE WILL HAVE TO TAKE PLACE UNDER THE **SAME CONDITIONS** AS THE LAST TIME.
SHERIFF
THAT MEANS WE RACE AT NIGHT!
HUH?
THAT'S NOT EXACTLY **FAIR,** SHERIFF.
SHERIFF
WE ALL KNOW MCQUEEN DOESN'T HAVE ANY **HEADLIGHTS.**
HE CAN'T RACE IN THE DARK!
OF COURSE, HE DOESN'T HAVE TO RACE ME AT ALL...
RUST-EZE
95
...IF HE THINKS HE CAN'T WIN.
OK, SHERIFF, IF THAT'S HOW YOU WANT IT, **I'M IN.** SEE YOU TONIGHT!
95
RUST-EZE

Flo's V8 Cafe
I'M READY FOR YOU *THIS* TIME, HOTSHOT.
I'M ALWAYS READY FOR SPEED NO MATTER WHAT TIME IT IS!
BUT WE SHOULDN'T JUST RACE FOR BRAGGING RIGHTS . . .
. . . THE LOSER WILL BUY A QUART OF OIL FOR EVERYONE!
I KNEW I LIKED THAT KID!
DEAL!
A FEW HOURS LATER...
READY?
YOU BET, DOC!
I'LL BE WAITING FOR YOU AT THE FINISH LINE, CHAMP.
GO!
VROOOM

I'M IN THE LEAD!
I'M ALMOST SORRY TO EMBARRASS THE HOT ROD LIKE THIS, BUT...
...HUH?
VROOOOOOOOM
HEY, SHERIFF! DID YOU STOP FOR GAS?
GASP! YOU WON--AGAIN! I GUESS I CAN'T COMPETE WITH A PISTON CUP CIRCUIT RACER.
HOW DID YOU *DO* IT?

SARGE'S NIGHT VISION GOGGLES DEFINITELY HELPED. THANKS, SARGE!
A PLEASURE, PRIVATE!
HA HA! THAT'LL TEACH ME TO TALK BIG.
YOU GAVE IT YOUR BEST, SHERIFF--THE OIL'S ON ME.
OR REALLY, ON THE BILL OF MY AGENT, HARV.
THAT'S TALKING LIKE A CHAMP!
LATER . . .
YOU'RE NOT BAD AT ALL, SHERIFF! WHY DON'T YOU TAKE UP RACING?
AND WHAT ABOUT YOU? HAVE YOU EVER THOUGHT OF BECOMING DEPUTY SHERIFF?
OF COURSE, YOU WOULD HAVE TO WORK THE DAY SHIFT!
THE END!

WRITER: CARLOTTA QUATTROCOLO PENCILS: VALENTINO FORLINI INKS: SONIA MATRONE COLOR: VALENTINO FORLINI LETTERS: JOHN GREEN

HEY!
DON'T WORRY, FELLERS, I KNOW THE PITS LIKE THE BACK OF MY HOOD!
EASY IDLE A Warm Start To A Cold Morning
HEY, MAN, I'M ALL FOR IT!
SPLURT THAT'S COLD!
RPM Nighttime Backfire Suppr
AW, SHOOT. YOU'RE GONNA MA ME B
YEAH, HE IS A... UH... A "PRE-CISIONAL INSTRUMENT OF SPEED AND AERO-MATICS."
NOW YOU FELLERS ARE GONNA SEE WHAT A "RUSTY OLD TOW TRUCK" CAN DO!
WOW...
YOU CAN COUNT ON ME!
I'M ALWAYS READY FOR SPEED NO MATTER WHAT TIME IT IS!
SPEED! AM SPEED!
GO!
HUH
I KNEW I LIKED THAT KID!
GONNA TONIC
Leak Less ADULT DRIP PANS
No Stall
WELCOME BACK TO THE PIT CREW!
GREAT, KID. IT'S TIME FOR PIT STOP.
© Disney/Pixar

"...FOR SOME STYLE!"
PIT STOP!
STANLEY WAS **SO** PERSISTENT! FINALLY I SAID, "ALL RIGHT! **ONE** LITTLE DATE..."
COOL! THANKS, GUYS. I DON'T KNOW WHAT I WOULD HAVE DONE WITHOUT YOU!
WHAT PLANS DO YOU HAVE FOR TONIGHT, ANYWAY?
PLANS?! WITH ALL THIS **FUSS** I FORGOT TO MAKE ANY!

DON'T WORRY! I'M GREAT AT PLANNING DATES! UHM... YOU COULD TAKE HER FISHING...
I CAUGHT... SOMETHING?
YOU MIGHT EVEN FIND MY HOOD!
OR YOU COULD GO TRACTOR TIPPING...
SO THIS IS THE PLAN FOR THE EVENING?
UHM... MATER ALWAYS HAS FUN DOING THIS...
OR...
ACTUALLY, MATER, I THINK WE'LL JUST GO FOR A DRIVE AND POP IN AT FLO'S!
HUH? WAIT! WHAT ABOUT A LITTLE DIRT RACING?
THE END!

WRITER: MICHAEL STEWART PENCILS: FABIO POCHET INKS: RICCARDO SISTI COLOR: VALENTINO FORLINI LETTERS: MICHAEL STEWART

WHAT DO *YOU* THINK, DOC? IS THIS OLD PLACE WORTH *FIXING UP?*
WHY BOTHER? THEY JUST *DON'T* MAKE MOVIES LIKE THEY USED TO.
YEAH, NOW THEY HAVE ALL THAT *EXTRA* STUFF IN THEM--LIKE *SOUND* AND *COLOR.*
DON'T WORRY, SALLY.
MCQUEEN WILL THINK OF SOMETHIN'. RIGHT, BUDDY?
UH, YEAH. YEAH. DON'T WORRY, SALLY, I'VE GOT IT COVERED!
THANKS, STICKERS.
SOON...
MATER, I DON'T *HAVE* A PLAN TO CLEAR THE DRIVE-IN!
WELL, I'M SURE WE CAN THINK OF *SOMETHIN'*... I KNOW!
WE'LL GET BESSIE AND SOME OLD GAS CANS, AND WE'LL TUNNEL UNDER...
SIGH
WELL, HONK MY HORN! IT'S OUR *LUCKY DAY,* LIGHTNIN'!
THERE'S OUR PLAN RIGHT THERE. AND IT'LL BE FUU-*UN!*
HUH? ALL I SEE ARE *TRACTORS...*

HAW HAW! THERE'S NOTHIN' BETTER THAN TRACTOR TIPPING!
HONK!
!
BROOOAM!
HEH HEH. YOU'RE RIGHT ABOUT THAT, MATER.
BUT EXPLAIN TO ME WHAT THIS HAS TO DO WITH CLEANING UP THE DRIVE-IN.
SNORT!
UH... YOU'LL SEE. I THINK I HEAR HIM.
WHO?
YUP, THAT'S FRANK!
LET'S GO!
THIS PLAN IS DEFINITELY NOT FUN ANYMORE!
SOON...
I CAN'T BELIEVE THOSE TWO WENT TRACTOR TIPPING WHEN THERE'S SO MUCH WORK TO BE DONE!
JUST WATCH-- THEY MAY BE ON TO SOMETHING...
CHECK OUT THIS BACKWARDS DRIVING!
MATER, YOU'RE CRAZY! HE'S GETTING CLOSE!

LOOKY THERE, SEE. HE'S MOWIN' DOWN ALL THEM WEEDS. AIN'T WE SMART?
GREAT PLAN, MATER!
BUT IT ONLY WORKS IF HE DOESN'T CATCH US--
--SO QUIT YOUR FOOLIN'!
BUMP!
I WAS JUST HAVING A LITTLE FUN.
EXCELLENT WORK! THIS PLACE IS STARTING TO LOOK SHIPSHAPE!
FAREWELL, SWEET LITTLE WEEDS!
GOOD PLAN, BOYS! HOW ABOUT ONE MORE PASS?
COMIN' RIGHT UP, DOC. WOO-HOO!
EVENTUALLY...
I HOPE YOU HAVE A PLAN FOR DEALING WITH FRANK, NOW THAT THE WHOLE DRIVE-IN IS MOWED CLEAN.
SURE I DO! THIS IS PRETTY MUCH IT--
--WE JUST LET HIM CHASE US DOWN THE HIGHWAY AND HOPE THAT HE RUNS OUT OF GAS BEFORE WE DO!
SIGH
THE END!

Disney • PIXAR THE WORLD OF Cars

WRITER: ALESSANDRO SISTI PENCILS: VALENTINO FORLINI INKS: RAFFAELLA SECCIA COLOR: VALENTINO FORLINI LETTERS: JOHN GREEN

YOU CAN SEE FOR YOURSELF. I'M ARRESTING MCQUEEN!
WHAT FOR? WHAT DID HE DO WRONG?
SHERIFF
I DON'T KNOW WHAT'S GOTTEN INTO DOC, BUT HE WENT THROUGH HIS OLD LAW BOOK...
"...AND DISCOVERED A BUNCH OF FORGOTTEN LOCAL RULES."
A-HA!
LIKE CODE 6906--IT IS PROHIBITED IN RADIATOR SPRINGS TO DRIVE WITHOUT HEADLIGHTS AND A HORN!
APPARENTLY MY HEADLIGHT STICKERS DON'T COUNT, AND I DON'T HAVE A HORN.
PLUS, CODE 61006-- HIS ENGINE IS TOO POWERFUL... AND PLENTY OF OTHER DETAILS.
SO DOC HAS DECIDED TO PUT HIM ON TRIAL IMMEDIATELY!
THAT'S CRAZY!

SOON . . .
IT MAY BE CRAZY, BUT IT'S THE **LAW!**
THEN **I'LL** DEFEND HIM.
IMPOSSIBLE! YOU'RE THE PROSECUTOR.
ACCUSED
SHERIFF
NOT THIS TIME.
I CAN REPLACE YOU, HONEY!
ORDER IN THE COURT! SALLY, DON'T MAKE ME CHARGE YOU WITH CONTEMPT. **LIZZIE**, TAKE YOUR PLACE WITH THE ACCUSED.
LET THE TRIAL BEGIN.
MATER? DO YOU HEAR SOME HOTROD SPEEDERS OUT THERE?
UM, YEAH... WE BETTER GO CATCH 'EM. LET'S GO!
I DON'T BELIEVE THIS. THIS IS CRAZY, **DOC!** HE CAN'T HAVE A FAIR TRIAL UNDER THESE CONDITIONS. IF YOU WANT TO TALK LAW CODES, THEN...
SHERIFF
TIRES
COME ON, QUICK!
THEY'LL BE THERE FOR A WHILE.

MEANWHILE...
DOES THE DEFENDANT PLEAD GUILTY OR INNOCENT?
IF ONLY STANLEY WERE HERE, YOU'D ANSWER HIM!
WHAT SORT OF A QUESTION IS THAT, DOC?
I REMEMBER EYEING STANLEY FROM ACROSS THE COURTROOM. HE WAS A HANDSOME DEVIL...
LIZZIE? STAY WITH ME HERE...
ONCE HE ASKED ME TO BE HIS DATE AT A PARTY. HEY, WHEN IS THAT PARTY ANYWAY?
PARTY? WHAT PARTY?
LIZZIE MEANT IT WOULD BE A REAL PARTY FOR CRIMINALS IF THE LAW WERE NOT RESPECTED!
OF COURSE! EXACTLY!

ELSEWHERE...
GRAND OPENING
LET'S HURRY UP!
THE TRIAL WON'T LAST FOREVER!
IN FACT...
DOC! LOOK!
UH... WELL, THE COURT CLOSES AT 4 O'CLOCK. TIME'S UP.
THE CASE IS CLOSED! I PRONOUNCE THE DEFENDANT... *GUILTY!*
WHAAAT?!?
YOU'RE WRONG! I WON'T STAND FOR THIS!
CLANG!
IF YOU WANT TO THROW ME IN JAIL, YOU'LL HAVE TO *CATCH* ME FIRST!
QUICK, LET'S *FOLLOW* HIM!
WAIT FOR ME!
WHERE ARE THEY GOING? IT LOOKS LIKE THEY'RE HEADING...

...TOWARD THE WHEEL WELL?
FOR SHE'S A JOLLY GOOD FELLOW, FOR SHE'S...
DID YOU FORGET WHAT DAY IT IS TODAY?
OH? I...
IT'S THE ANNIVERSARY OF YOUR ARRIVAL IN RADIATOR SPRINGS!
WE WANTED TO THROW YOU A PARTY AT THE SPOT YOU LOVE THE MOST-- WHICH WAS RIGHT HERE.
BUT WE HAD TO KEEP YOU AWAY TO DECORATE IT PROPERLY!
SO YOU SET UP THAT FAKE TRIAL? WHOSE IDEA WAS IT?
SINCE I AM THE JUDGE, I CAN CONFESS... WE ARE ALL GUILTY!
HEY, MY ACTING WAS PRETTY GOOD, HUH? MCQUEEN, YOU THINK I COULD GET A PART IN ONE OF THOSE BIG MOVIES?
MATER...
THE END!

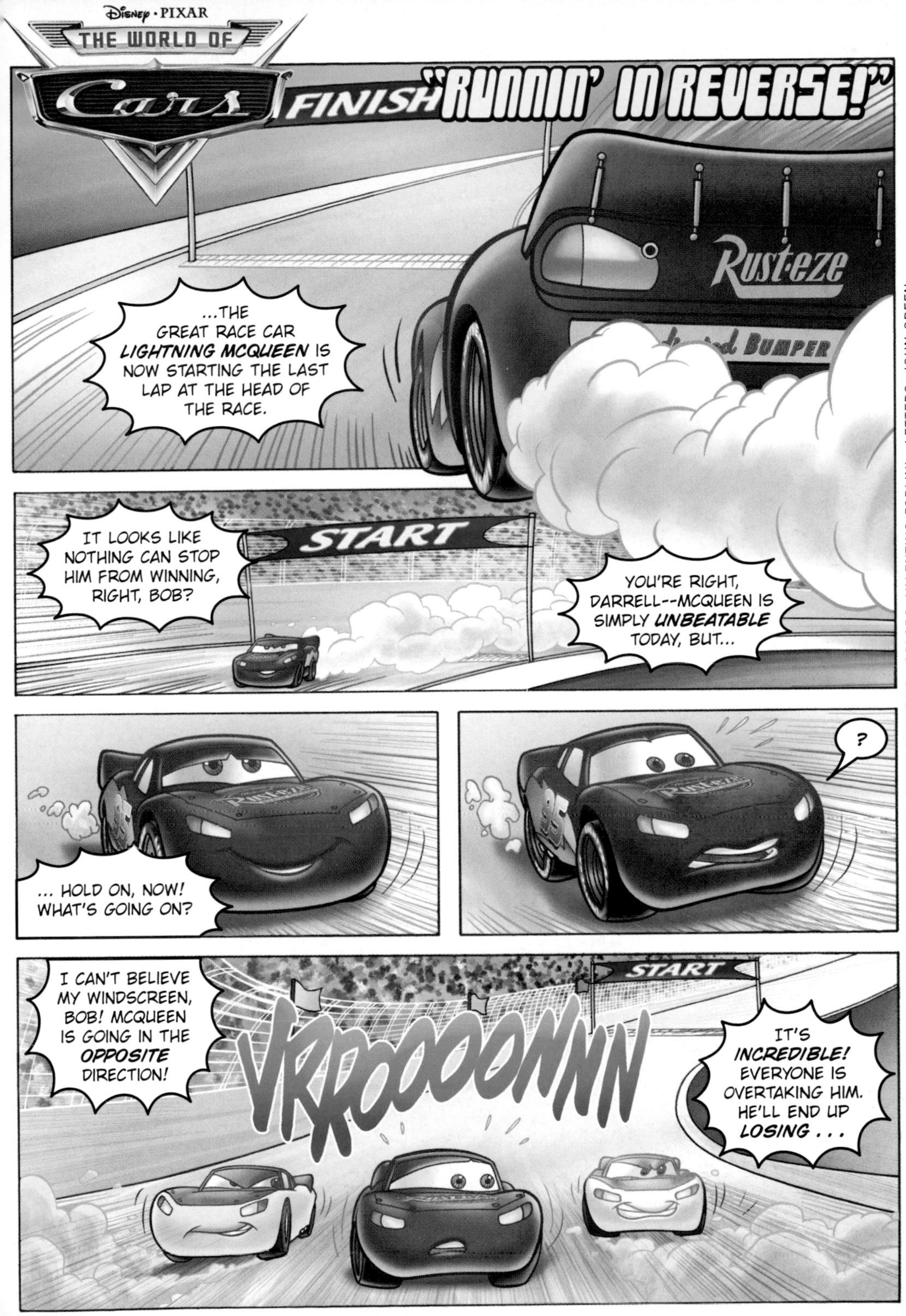

WRITER: ALESSANDRO FERRARI PENCILS: VALENTINO FORLINI INKS: SONIA MATRONE COLORS: VALENTINO FORLINI LETTERS: JOHN GREEN

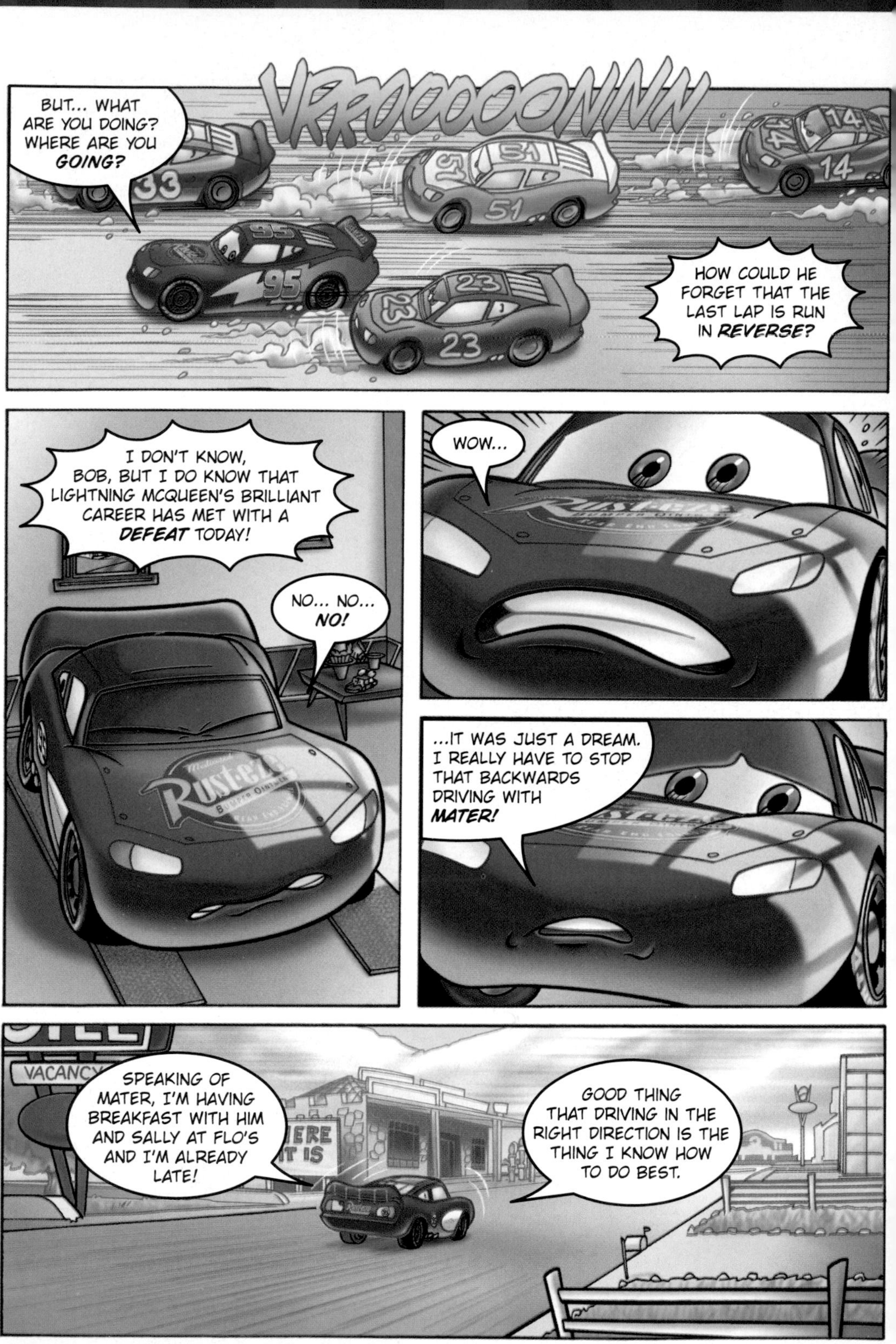
VRROOOOONNNN
BUT... WHAT ARE YOU DOING? WHERE ARE YOU GOING?
HOW COULD HE FORGET THAT THE LAST LAP IS RUN IN REVERSE?
I DON'T KNOW, BOB, BUT I DO KNOW THAT LIGHTNING McQUEEN'S BRILLIANT CAREER HAS MET WITH A DEFEAT TODAY!
NO... NO... NO!
WOW...
...IT WAS JUST A DREAM. I REALLY HAVE TO STOP THAT BACKWARDS DRIVING WITH MATER!
VACANCY
SPEAKING OF MATER, I'M HAVING BREAKFAST WITH HIM AND SALLY AT FLO'S AND I'M ALREADY LATE!
GOOD THING THAT DRIVING IN THE RIGHT DIRECTION IS THE THING I KNOW HOW TO DO BEST.

SCREEEK
Flo's Cafe
HEY THERE, BUDDY, HOW'S IT GOING? HEE HEE HEE...
GOOD MORNING!
HEEEY, MCQUEEN--RELAX, MAN! FALL INTO THE RHYTHM!
HONK!
MATER? DOC? FILLMORE? RED?!?
HEY, STICKERS... WHERE ARE YOU RACING FORWARD TO?
OH NO, NOT YOU, TOO, SALLY!

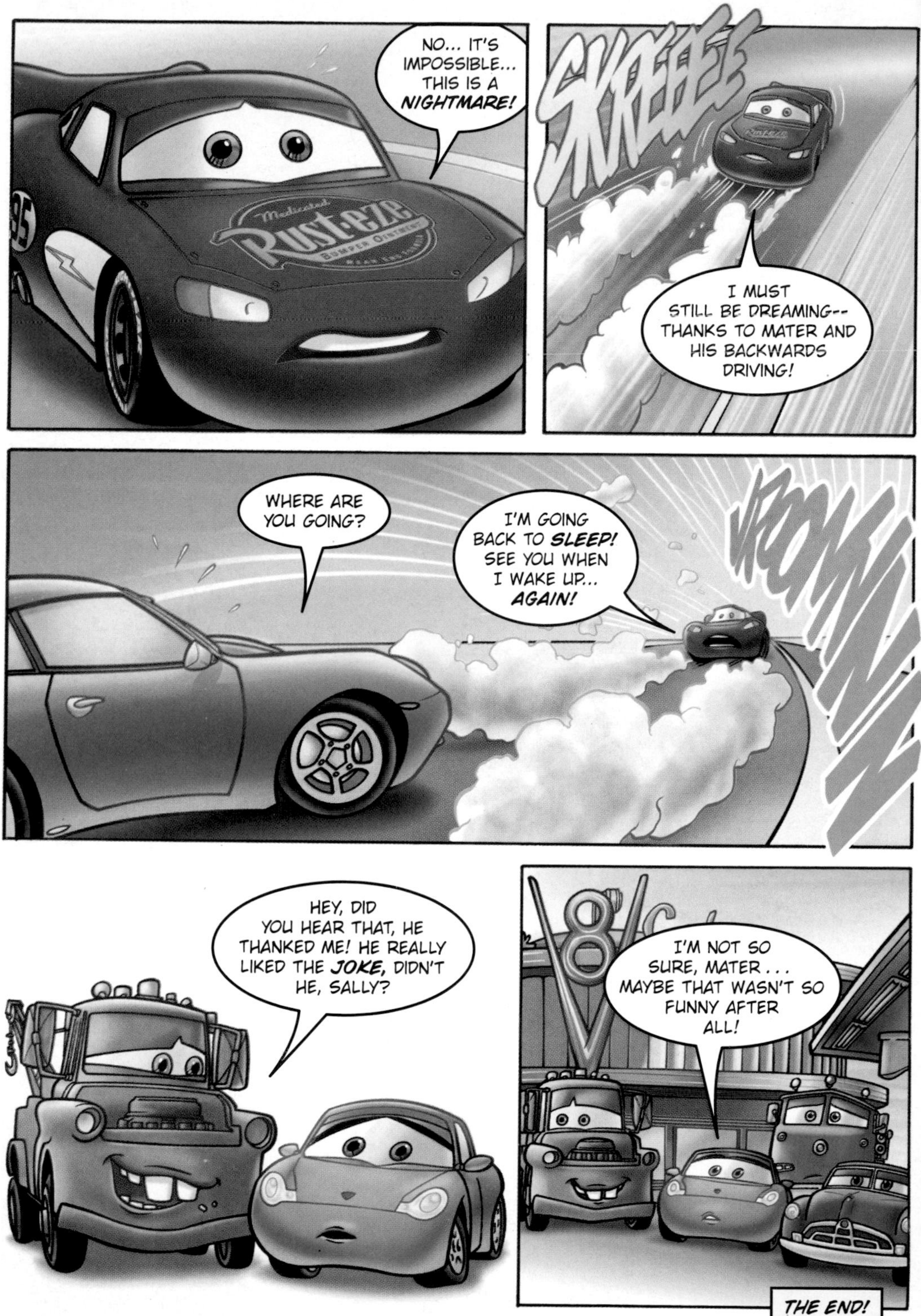
NO... IT'S IMPOSSIBLE... THIS IS A NIGHTMARE!
I MUST STILL BE DREAMING-- THANKS TO MATER AND HIS BACKWARDS DRIVING!
WHERE ARE YOU GOING?
I'M GOING BACK TO SLEEP! SEE YOU WHEN I WAKE UP... AGAIN!
HEY, DID YOU HEAR THAT, HE THANKED ME! HE REALLY LIKED THE JOKE, DIDN'T HE, SALLY?
I'M NOT SO SURE, MATER . . . MAYBE THAT WASN'T SO FUNNY AFTER ALL!
THE END!